Off We Go!

A Bear and Mole Story

Will Hillenbrand

Holiday House / New York

To Nina and Pam, I think you can.
—W. H.

Copyright © 2013 by Will Hillenbrand
All Rights Reserved
HOLIDAY HOUSE is registered in the U.S. Patent and Trademark Office.
Printed and Bound in August 2013 at Worzalla, Stevens Point, WI, U.S.A.
The illustrations were created in mixed media.
The typeface is Joel1.
www.holidayhouse.com

3 5 7 9 10 8 6 4

Library of Congress Cataloging in Publication Data
Hillenbrand, Will.
Off we go! : a Bear and Mole story / Will Hillenbrand. — First edition.
pages cm
Summary: "Bear teaches his friend, Mole, how to ride his bike with no training wheels. After many bumps
along the road, they make it to their final destination: the Storymobile"— Provided by publisher.
ISBN 978-0-8234-2520-4 (hardcover)
[1. Bicycles and bicycling—Fiction. 2. Bears—Fiction. 3. Moles (Animals)—Fiction.]
I. Title.   PZ7.H55773Of 2013   E—dc23   2012045823

Bear picked books off the shelf.

He put them in a bag.

"Ready, Mole?" asked Bear.

"Bear, I need some help," replied Mole.

Mole grinned.
"These need to come off.
I'm riding today!"
he declared.

They removed.

Bear checked.

Mole tugged.

They hoisted.

Mole packed.

Mole snapped.

At last Mole was ready.

Mole kicked off.
Bear pushed.

Wobble.
Wobble.
Wobble.

TODAY!

Crash.

Mole sobbed, "I quit."

"I think you can," encouraged Bear.

"You do?"

Mole took a deep
breath and
wiped his eyes.

Ready, OFF WE GO!

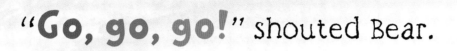
"**Go, go, go!**" shouted Bear.

"**Faster, faster, faster,**" said Mole.

"You're doing it!" whooped Bear.

Bump. Bump. Bump.

"Whoa, whoa!" exhaled Mole.

"Look out!" shouted Bear.

"Oh dear!" Bear grimaced.

"Look OUT!" called Bear.

"Oh no." Bear sighed.

"I did it!"
hollered Mole.

"You certainly did,"
said Bear with a smile.